a good day's fishing

a good day's fishing

by
james prosek

SIMON & SCHUSTER BOOKS FOR YOUNG READERS

New York London Toronto Sydney Singapore

SIMON & SCHUSTER
BOOKS FOR YOUNG READERS
An imprint of Simon & Schuster
Children's Publishing Division
1230 Avenue of the Americas
New York, New York 10020

SIMON & SCHUSTER BOOKS FOR
YOUNG READERS is a trademark of
Simon & Schuster, Inc.
Book design by Lee Wade
The text for this book is set in Mrs. Eaves.
The illustrations for this book are
rendered in watercolors.
Manufactured in China
10 9 8 7 6 5 4 3 2
Library of Congress Cataloging-in-
Publication Data
Prosek, James, 1975-
A good day's fishing / James Prosek.
p. cm.
Summary: A child searches through the
hooks, lures, bobbers, and other
paraphernalia in his tackle box for the
one thing he needs to ensure a good day's
fishing. Includes a detailed glossary.
ISBN 0-689-85327-0
[1. Fishing—Fiction. 2. Fishing tackle—
Fiction.]
I. Title.
PZ7.P94348 Go 2004
[E]—dc21
2003007383

first edition

FOR ARJUNA

This is my tackle box.
What I need for a
good day's fishing is
in here somewhere!

It's not this. . . .

This is a spinner.

It spins around and

attracts fish's attention.

I used it to catch . . .

a yellow perch.

And this is a phoebe spoon.
It flashes in the water.

I caught a pumpkinseed sunfish on it
in old Farmer Kachele's pond.

I hooked a crappie, too,
but it got away!

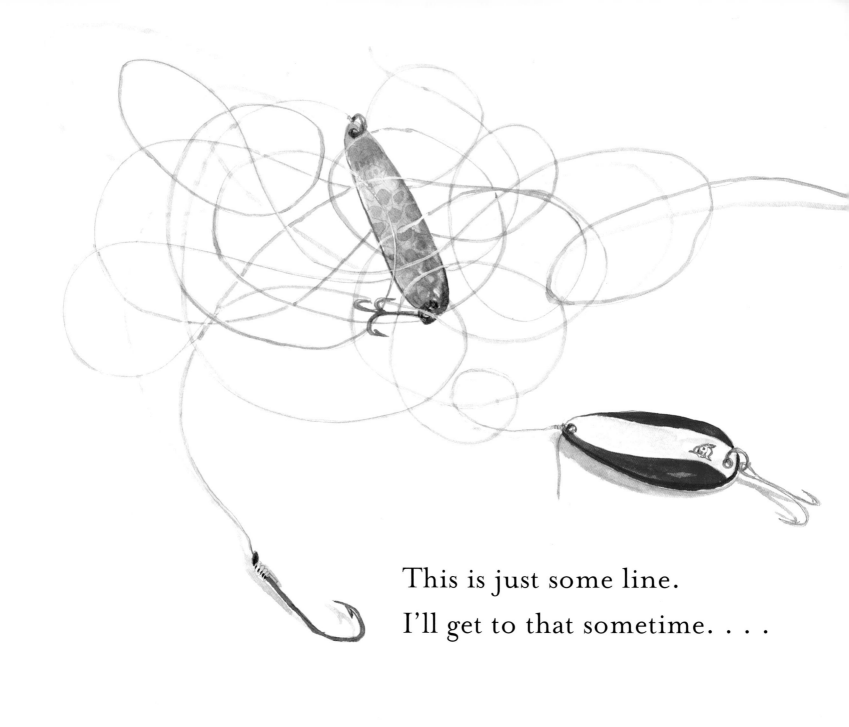

This is just some line.

I'll get to that sometime. . . .

These are my bobbers and swivels,
to make things float.

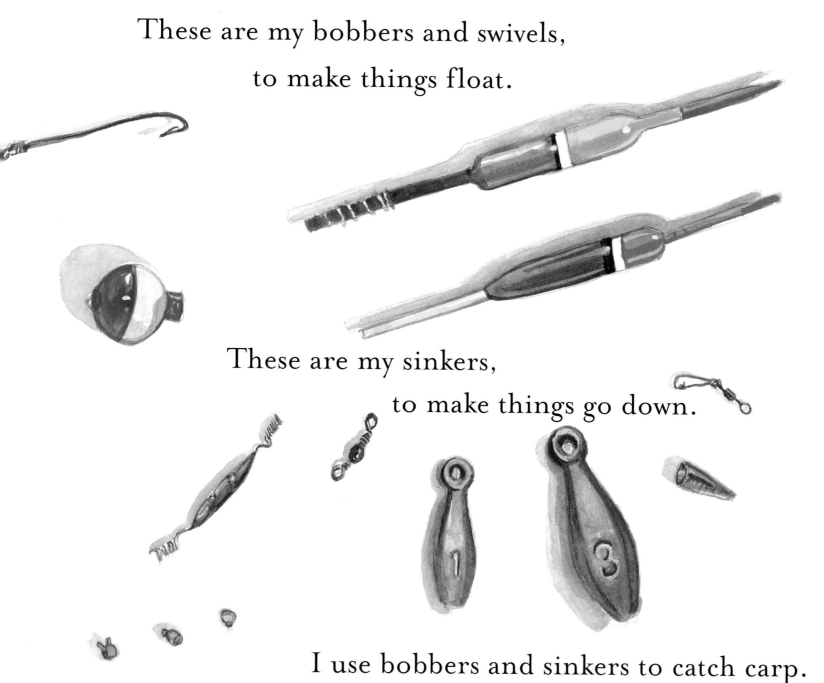

These are my sinkers,
to make things go down.

I use bobbers and sinkers to catch carp.

And here are my hooks.

Aren't they cool?

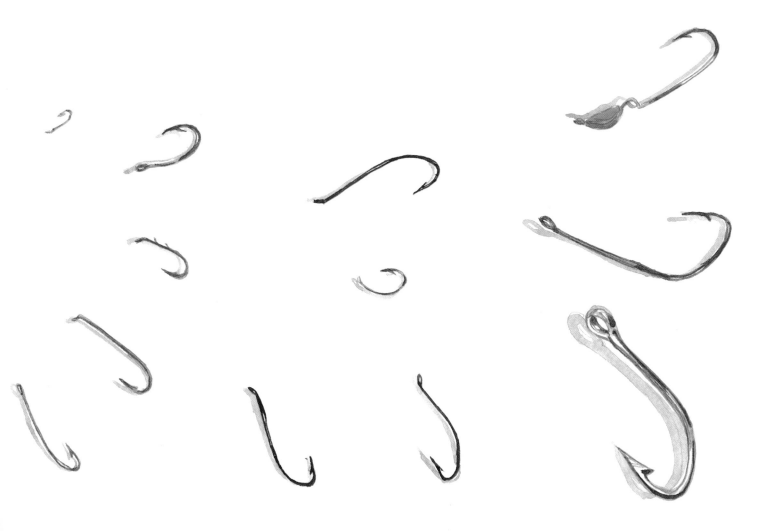

Here's an old sandwich.
What was I looking for again?

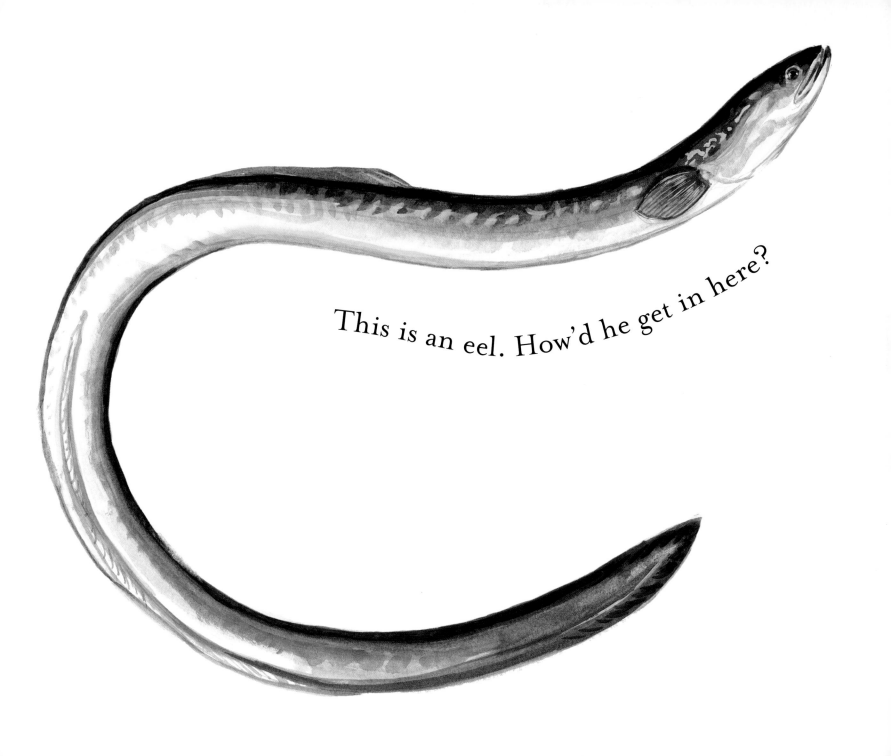

This is an eel. How'd he get in here?

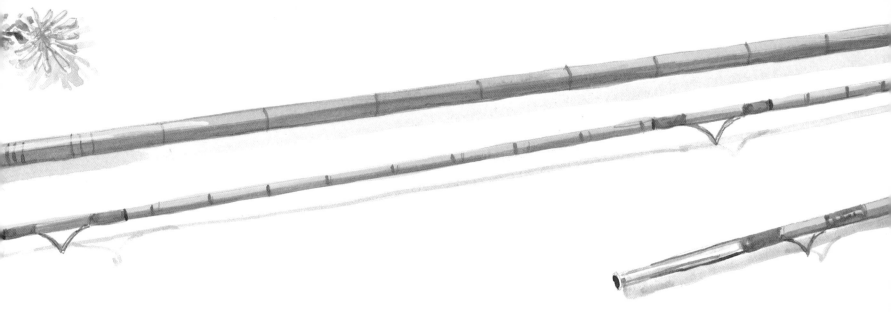

Here's my fly rod
and fly reel and

my rubber fish lure.

I never get anything on that!

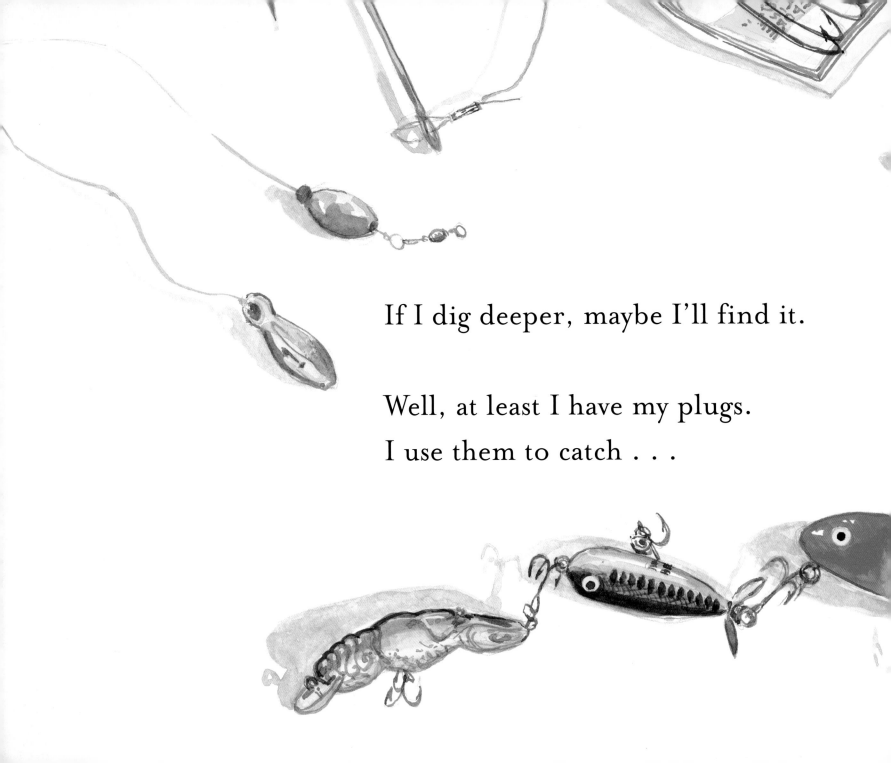

If I dig deeper, maybe I'll find it.

Well, at least I have my plugs.
I use them to catch . . .

largemouth bass.

And these are my flies,
tied from furs and feathers.

They're for catching

my favorite fish . . .

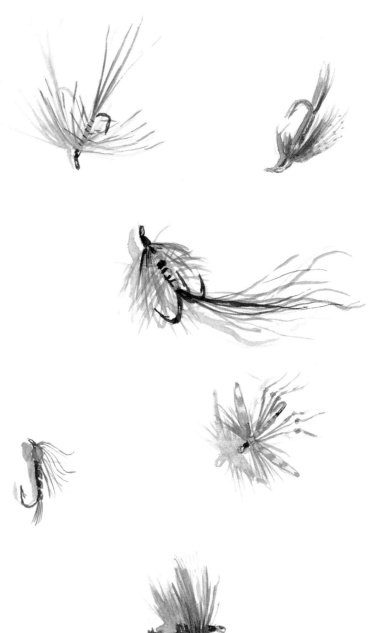

brook trout.

What I really
need isn't my
wrench or my
tape measure

or my lucky lure.

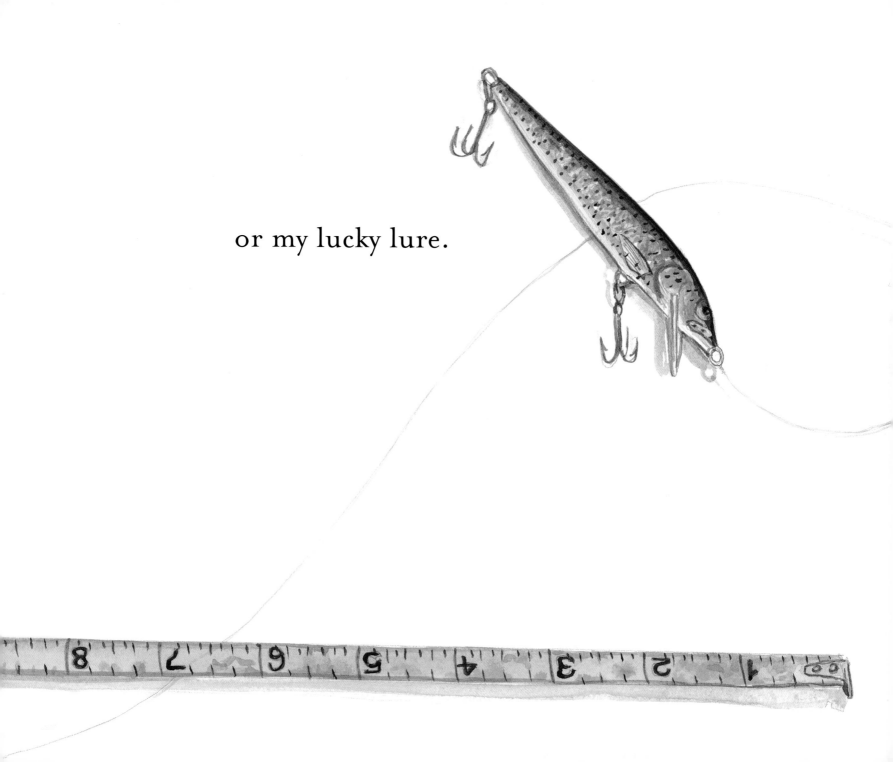

It's my hat.

LURE AND FLY GLOSSARY

The first rule of fishing is that there are no rules (except, of course, to be careful with the hooks), but it helps to know a few basic things. This lure and fly glossary is intended to help the young, and not so young, learn the basic vocabulary of fishing. Lures are colorful and fun to collect—as appealing to fishermen and fisherwomen as they are to fish.

In catching fish it helps to know the fish's habits and in what kinds of places they like to live. Most fish, for instance, like to hang out near some kind of structure. Just as we prefer to have a roof over our heads, a place where we feel protected, fish like to hide under logs or behind rocks, places where they feel concealed and from which they can ambush their food. There is a lot to know about fish and the way they live—you can never know it all—and that's why fishing is a pastime that can keep you interested for a lifetime.

LURES

Fish feed by sight, by feel, and by smell. Lures don't usually have a smell, so they have to make up for this with lots of flash and movement. Fish can detect movement even if they don't see the lure, feeling it through a sensory organ along their sides called a "lateral line."

The larger the mouth of the fish you are after, the larger the lure you want to use. In this way fishing is very logical, although occasionally a very small fish will eat a lure bigger than itself, or a very large fish will eat a tiny lure. You will find these things out with experience. Spending time on the water is the only way to become an effective fisherman or fisherwoman (unless you were born lucky).

SPINNERS

A spinner attracts fish with a small metal blade that spins around the shaft and flashes in the water. The flash excites fish because it resembles a wounded baitfish, its silver sides shining in the water. The fish not only sees the flash of the spinner but feels the vibration of the blade spinning in the water. That is why spinners work as well in muddy, low-visibility water as they do in clear water with good visibility. Spinners in different sizes can catch just about any kind of fish.

Standard spinners

The standard spinner is my favorite lure for small-stream trout fishing. With a standard spinner, I generally use just a simple-and-straight retrieve, as opposed to stop-and-go. Rooster Tails and Mepps are classic types of spinners that work well.

standard spinner

SPINNERBAITS

A spinnerbait is a large lure that is a kind of hybrid between a spinner and a jig. (You can read about jigs on the next page.) It's a great lure for largemouth bass and pike, which are attracted by the commotion it makes. It's a good lure for fishing weedy areas.

spinnerbait

PLUGS

Minnow plugs

The floating minnow plug imitates a wounded minnow on the surface of the water. Fish are attracted to wounded prey—whether it is a minnow, a frog, or a large insect—because it is easier for them to catch and eat. (The most famous of the minnow plugs is one made by a company in Finland called Rapala. No tackle box—of mine, anyway—is complete without Rapala minnow plugs in different sizes.) When using a minnow plug, it is good to try different retrieves: Cast it out—pull it—stop—retrieve for a bit—stop again. Its clear plastic lip causes the plug to dive under the surface of the water. If it is a sinking plug, then the clear plastic lip makes the lure wobble. An irregular retrieve is good because it makes the minnow plug look like easy prey for a big fat fish.

minnow plug

Stick baits

A stick bait floats and also imitates a wounded creature struggling across the surface of the water. You just cast it and jerk and jiggle it across the surface, making a commotion. It is a good lure to use just before sunset on a warm summer night—especially for bass and pike.

stick bait

Propeller baits

Another surface plug, a propeller bait is like a stick bait with a small propeller on the back and sometimes on the front. The propeller spins around and makes a wake in the water that attracts fish, which see from beneath the surface its silhouette against the sky. It is a fun lure to use at night

propeller bait

because you can hear it sputtering along until a big fish comes up and breaks the surface of the water to eat it.

Crawlers

crazy crawler

jitterbug

A crawler is yet another lure that brings fish to the surface by making a wake and a lot of noise.

Poppers

A popper likewise imitates an animal trying to cross the water, like a frog or a mouse or a wounded fish. When you pull it, it pushes the water and makes a popping sound. It is also a good lure to use in the dark, because you can hear the lure and also the fish when it splashes out of the water to take it. Like all lures, poppers have great and unusual brand names (meant to attract the fisherman and fisherwoman). One of my favorites has always been the Hula Popper.

Hula Popper

Crankbaits

A crankbait is a plug that dips beneath the surface of the water. Its clear plastic lip causes it to go down as you pull it, and to wobble back and forth. Some crankbaits sink and some float. When I use a floating crankbait, I like to retrieve it, stop to let it float a bit, and then retrieve it again. Sometimes the fish takes it as it is floating to the surface. Like all plugs, crankbaits come in all sizes.

crankbait

Vibrating plugs

A vibrating plug sinks and has beads or rattles inside its hollow body that make noise as you pull it through the water. The noise and the shape—like a small baitfish, especially a shad or an alewife—attract fish.

vibrating plug

SOFT PLASTIC LURES

Rubber worms

Rubber worms are made of soft plastic that is molded into different shapes and sizes. There are many different ways to "rig," or put a rubber worm on, a hook. One is the standard rig, by threading the worm, top first, on to the hook. Another popular rig is called the Texas rig, where you thread the worm a little bit, slide the worm up toward the eye of the hook, and then turn the hook and imbed the point into the worm. This way the point of the hook is not exposed and you can pull it through the weeds without it getting hung up. When a fish strikes, the hook pushes through the plastic and into the fish's mouth.

I like to cast out a rubber worm, Texas rigged, let it sink to the bottom, and crawl it back slowly. This is especially effective in cold water, when the fish are sluggish.

Rubber worm hook

standard rig

Texas rig

standard rigging

1. 2. 3. 4. 5.

Texas rigging

1. 2. 3.

Rubber frog lures

There are all kinds of lures molded from plastic into lifelike shapes. This frog lure floats, and the hook points are above the frog so they don't get caught in the lily pads.

frog lure

JIGS

The jig is perhaps the most versatile of all lures. You can use it in shallow or deep water and in any size for any kind of fish. You can bounce it on the bottom or suspend it from a boat. The head of a jig is usually lead, and when you "jig" it through the water, the up-and-down motion

shad dart

bucktail jig

rubber jig

is appealing to fish. The basic idea of a top-heavy lure has also been applied to some types of flies for fly-fishing. Some jigs are made with deer hair tied to them (e.g., the bucktail jig and the shad dart), others with feathers (e.g., the crappie jig, which has soft down feathers called marabou). You can also rig a rubber worm on to a jig. Jigs are a good lure to use while ice fishing because they work when retrieved vertically, unlike plugs that usually must be fished horizontally, or across the surface.

crappie jig

SPOONS

The first spoon lure was probably made by attaching a hook to the head of an actual kitchen spoon. Spoons work in the same way that spinners do, in that they usually have a silver or gold underside that flashes in the water and attracts fish. Spoons, however, usually wobble rather than spin. They can be cast out and retrieved or jigged a bit with a stop-and-go retrieve. The red-and-white Daredevil spoon is a classic lure like the Rapala plug and can usually be found in just about any fisherman's or fisherwoman's tackle box.

weedless spoon

Daredevil spoon

Krockodile spoon

Phoebe spoon

FLIES

The main difference between fishing with flies and fishing with lures is that in lure fishing the weight of the lure casts the line (the line is thin and clear and virtually weightless) and in fly-fishing the line casts the lure (fly line is coated with plastic and relatively thick and weighted, while the fly is very light). There are many kinds of flies, from tiny dry flies made to imitate small insects to large streamers made to imitate larger insects such as dragonflies.

In fly-fishing the casting of the fly is the first technique to master; then you learn the various ways to fish the fly. All it takes to learn how to cast is a little instruction and plenty of practice. I used to practice in my yard by trying to hit a target. Most fly-fishing for trout is done in streams and rivers, but lakes can be good for trout fishing too.

DRY FLIES

Made by tying fur and/or feathers to a hook with thread, a dry fly imitates a natural insect. The alternative to an artificial fly is an actual live fly, which is difficult to use and not very durable. Remarkably a large part of a trout's daily diet consists of dozens, if not hundreds, of small flies and nymphs. A dry fly floats on the surface and imitates an adult aquatic insect, such as a mayfly or caddis fly. Dry-fly–fishing is exciting because you get to see the fish come up to the surface and sip the fly, or swirl at it, breaking the surface of the water. Well-known and effective patterns are the royal wulff, the Adams, and the elk hair caddis.

standard dry fly

EMERGING MAYFLIES

As a fly fisher, you should learn a little bit about the life cycle of the insect you are trying to imitate. Most flies of interest to fishermen and fisherwomen start as larvae or nymphs on the bottom of the stream and at some point come to the surface and metamorphose into adult winged insects by breaking out of their skin, called an exoskeleton. The "emerger" imitates the fly in the middle of its metamorphosis, with its folded wings just breaking out of its shell.

emerging mayfly

NYMPHS

A nymph imitates the larval stage of the adult insect and is fished under the water. Most of a fish's diet consists of subsurface foods, like nymphs. Usually they are fished in the same manner as the adult mayfly, that is, cast up the river and allowed to float freely down the current as a natural insect might. This technique is called a "dead drift." When a fish eats the nymph, you see the end of your fly line move, twitch, or stop.

standard nymph

STREAMERS

A streamer imitates a larger food item, like a big insect larva (e.g., a hellgrammite), a leech, or a minnow. Usually the streamer is retrieved after being cast out by pulling back the fly line through one's fingers, an action called stripping, similar to the way that a lure is retrieved. Sometimes the fly is allowed to swing across the river after it has been cast out. Pictured here are two classic and favorite streamers, a Mickey Finn and a woolly bugger.

Mickey Finn

woolly bugger

WET FLIES

A wet fly is like a streamer, but it is usually not pulled or stripped through the water; instead it is cast across the stream and allowed to swing across the currents. Wet flies are also used for salmon. They can be fished well below the surface or can be skittered on top. Some wet flies, like the Hornberg, can be fished wet or dry. A few famous wet-fly patterns are the Parmachene Belle, the Jock Scott, and the black bear green butt.

salmon fly

traditional wet fly

TERRESTRIALS

Terrestrial flies imitate land insects, like grasshoppers, ants, and beetles. On windy days these land insects can be blown off leaves of trees and grasses into the water and eaten by hungry trout. Sometimes you see trout waiting right near the bank of the stream for terrestrial insects to fall in. Pictured here is a grasshopper fly, which would be cast out and allowed to float down the stream.

terrestrial grasshopper fly

POPPER FLIES

A popper fly works much in the way that a popper lure does. The body is usually made from cork, balsa wood, or plastic. Some feathers are tied to the back. You cast it out and "pop" or gurgle it through the water, trying to attract the attention of a fish, and hope that the fish eats it. It imitates things like frogs or struggling, wounded minnows.

popper fly

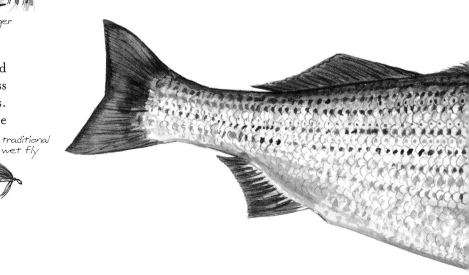